This igloo book belongs to:

....

KU-006-034

igloobooks

Published in 2017
by Igloo Books Ltd, Cottage Farm, Sywell, NN6 0BJ
www.igloobooks.com

Written by Nicky Lander
Illustrated by Kate Daubney

Cover designed by Lee Italiano
Interiors designed by Justine Ablett
Edited by Stephanie Moss

LEO002 0317
2 4 6 8 10 9 7 5 3 1
ISBN 978-1-78670-318-7

Printed and manufactured in China

SMELLY MONSTER

igloobooks

My best friend is my monster. He's as **smelly** as can be.
One day he was in the kitchen and he said, **"Play with me!"**

We spent the day together, getting **muddy**, **stinky** and **smelly**.
My monster even showed me how to make **wobbly** pink-worm jelly!

My monster likes to look his very best wherever he goes.
So he bathes in **Slimy** swamps and trims the green claws on his toes.

He smooths his hair with fish oil and cleans his teeth with **mouldy** goo.
He rubs old cheese under his arms and that smells **stinky**, too!

Once, my monster took a hot-air balloon trip.

UP and UP it soared.

But it wasn't long before my monster got **very, very** bored.

He picked a bogey from his nose, loaded his catapult and pulled back.
The bogey **flew** through the sky and hit the poor birds with a
thwack!

Sometimes he gets greasy spots. They're **squishy** and they're green.
When he's got a big one, you'll know exactly where he's been.

He loves to **squeeze** and **squash** them, then **squish** 'em, 'til they **spurt**.
He just can't wait to see how far that gross, green pus will **squirt!**

My monster loves to play pretend.
We do it all the time.
We imagine that we're pirates,
sailing on a sea of **slime.**

We have a cross-bones flag and my monster wears a smelly vest.
We battle **scary** sea monsters for their stinky-treasure chest.

He wears the **wackiest** outfits. They're the **worst** I've ever seen.

Last year at my birthday party, his shorts were **snot-slime** green.

His hat was covered in toothy bats and curly, pink mouse tails.

His top was made of chewing gum, complete with shells and snails!

My monster gets **awful** wind. It makes such a **terrible** smell.
Not only does it stink, but it powers his cart, as well!
He loves to **whizz** on by, as the **whiff** fills up the air.
His friends all hold their noses and can't help but stop and stare.

Whenever we go on holiday, my monster never behaves.
Last year we even got lost together in some dark and **grimy** caves.

He **stomped** in lots of sandcastles and I always got the blame.
But I know a holiday without him just wouldn't be the same.

Lately he's been learning how to ride my bright red bike.
I love showing him the things that I know he'll really like.
He covers the ramp in slime and waves as he **whooshes** by.
That's one monster trick I'm not quite brave enough to try.

I know my monster likes **revolting** stuff,
like **furry** moths and slugs.

And he loves to suck the

goo

from lots of different
sorts of bugs.

But even though he's imaginary and really just pretend,
he'll always be my **super-smelly**, very **best**, best friend.